AF138708

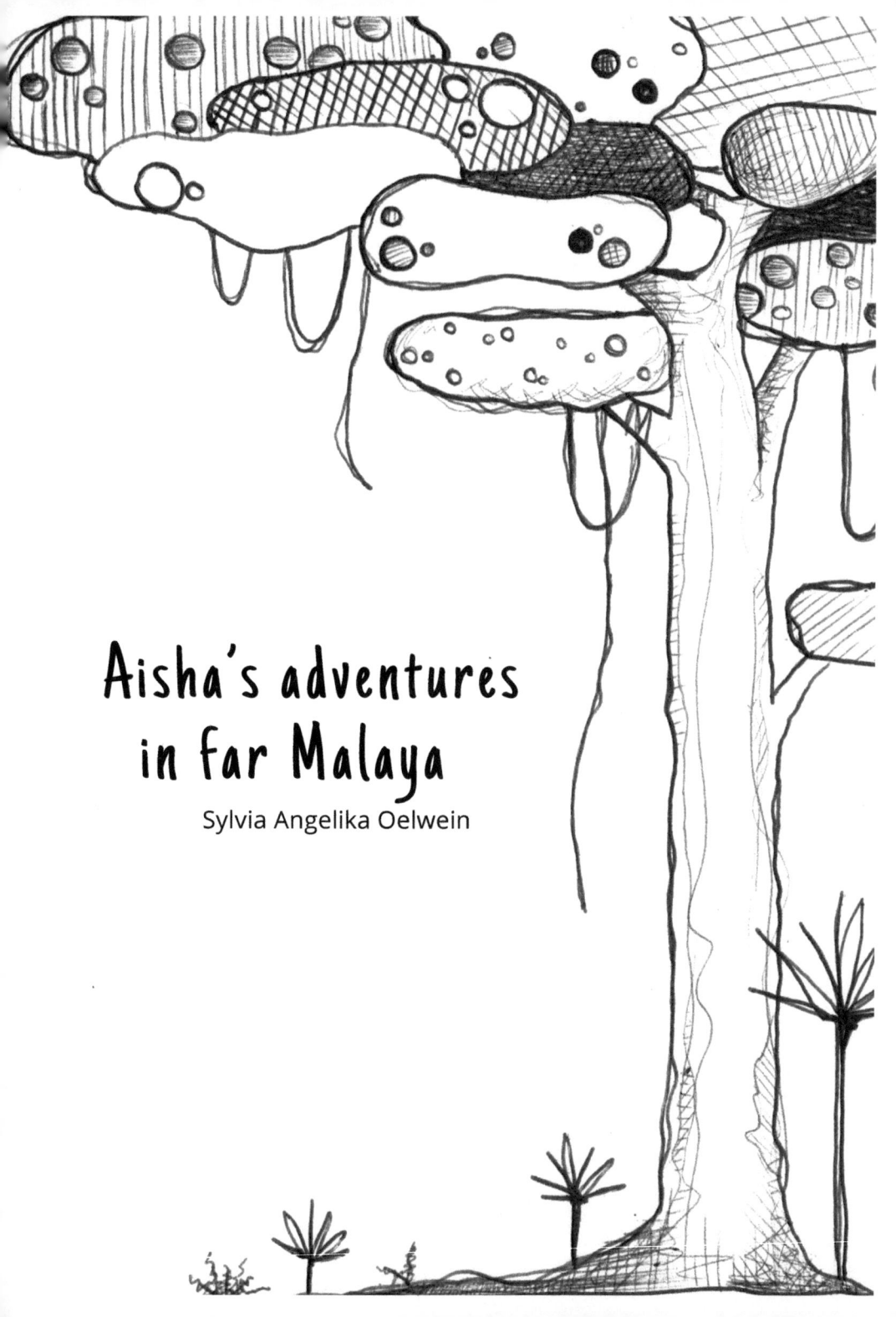

Aisha's adventures in far Malaya

Sylvia Angelika Oelwein

Sylvia Angelika Oelwein

Aisha's adventures in far Malaya

Animal stories for children age five and up as well as adults who have not forgotten the magic of seeing things through children's eyes.

Bibliografische Information der Deutschen Nationalbibliothek
Die Deutsche Nationalbibliothek verzeichnet diese Publikation in der
Deutschen Nationalbibliografie; detaillierte bibliografische Daten sind im
Internet über http://dnb.d-nb.de abrufbar.

More information about the author:
Email: Sylvia.oelwein@gmail.com
Tel. 0049-163 7302237
Translator: Sylvia Angelika Oelwein
Lecture: Sylvester Schreitmüller, Owatonna, USA
Design: Raymond Eiber
Illustrations: Jan Anderson

© Copyright: Sylvia Angelika Oelwein 2015
All rights reserved.

Printed and published:
BoD - Books on Demand, Norderstedt

ISBN: 9-783738642759

This book is dedicated to a special child, my first grandchild, and also to the parents, my son Philipp and his wife Angelina; as well as to my daughters Isabel, and Julia and their families; and to all the children of the world!

My wish is that this book will connect the people to nature more than ever before, to the plants, animals in our planet. We all hope for a peaceful and happy future so that nature can be kept alive, animals are able to live in their natural habitat, humans live in peace and respect each other no matter what culture they belong to and which language they speak.

Contents

Preface

There are not many adults who are able to think like a child and feel the phantasy that they often experience. We adults complicate life too much and thus lose the relationship that goes with their age.

But what can we people do without relating to the world around us?
Has our relationship to the world around us not always been the example for our technical development and has served the people? Have we not copied nature in many ways? We will never succeed our attempts to replace nature completely.

Let`s go take a walk into the forest, to be exact, on the east coast of Malaya and the jungle. (Malaya is the old name for Malaysia).

A good old friend told me some 25 years ago: watch the birds, they live simply, they do not sew, they do not harvest, they just spread their wings and fly. That is true freedom!

Now enjoy reading these animal stories, which I have experienced in the world around me and have written for children. But just maybe there are some adults out there who will also enjoy them.

Kuantan, Malaya, January 2015

Aisha

Aisha is a young 7-year-old girl living in a Kampong (small village) with her parents and three brothers. The Kampong is located outside of the town called Sungai Lembing, and so Aisha spent much time wandering around their surroundings.

Her brothers were not interested in their surroundings. They were older than she was, except her little brother Zainiffa accompanied her once in a while as she explained to him the world around her.

Zainiffa was 10 years old and already attended high school in Kuantan. His brother Mohamed was 13 and Ibrahim was already 15 years old. Both the older brothers have almost finished school and were waiting to get out for a workplace in Kuala Lumpur. But there was not enough work for everyone.

Mohamed would like to work as a mechanic, Ibrahim wanted to drive a big bus. Zainiffa dreamt of becoming a famous painter one day.

Father worked in a resort as a caretaker and mother did some sewing work for different people in order to earn some extra money. As a matter of fact there would have been enough work in the house; but to feed 5 hungry mouths she had to work a little more!

Life in the Kampong was simple. They had all they needed: water, a generator, gas for cooking and a bed for everyone. The three brothers shared a room and there was an extra room for Aisha, because she was a girl!

They had a dog, Josef and two cats, Teluk und Baluk. Five chickens were also running around which supplied the family with eggs. And when one egg hatched and the little chick was big enough to lay eggs, one of the bigger ones was used for dinner... well, that was Kampong life; the family had to survive and to do what was necessary. Thus there remained always five hens.

Of course many monkeys lived nearby and sometimes it happened that a banana or some nuts were taken! Mother was not very happy about this; she wanted these things for dinner.

Because of this Aisha had many unusual adventures. Some of them I wish to tell you about.

The little crab Ketam

Early one morning Aisha went to the sea as usual to wash her feet. She liked being alone at the seashore, before mother called her for breakfast and would take her to school.

It was low tide. So she had to walk far onto the ocean before she reached the water.

"Watch out where you step!" someone said, "you`ll step right onto my head!"

Aisha turned around surprised and frightened at the same time, but she did not see anyone. She looked all over, but still no one. So she looked onto the ground between her feet and suddenly discovered a little crab. It was of the same color as the sand, so she had not noticed before. This little crab peeped out of this hole and looked up at her.

Aisha kneeled down and asked:" what is your name?"

"Ketam is my name, and what is yours?"

"I am Aisha", she replied.

Then she noticed the wonderful drawings, which the little animal made digging sand out of the hole. He was not bigger than her thumbnail. "How wonderful!" she called out loudly filled with joy, "this is a drawing!"

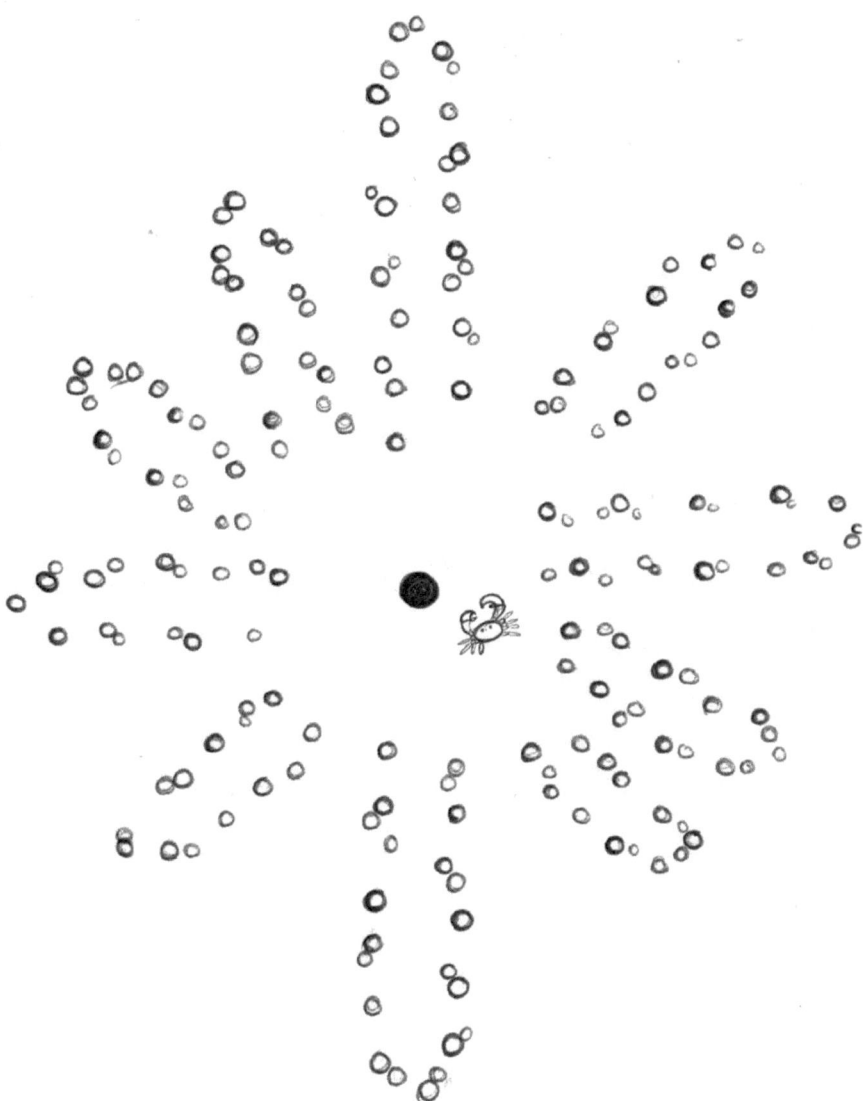

In fact, this little crab has dug a hole which is lots of work: he dug all the sand out of his hole and distributed it around the hole. This made the hole useful to him to hide when necessary.

Around the hole Aisha saw the most beautiful drawings, which even looked like a star, formed with little sand balls.
With joy and interest Aisha regarded his artistic abilities and said: "You are an artist! How did you create this artwork? I would not even been able to draw this onto a single piece of paper!"

The little crab gave her a big smile, his whole face basically lit up and both his pincers he lifted up with joy! "Yes, "he said proudly, "I`ve been working on this all morning. And now you have come and destroyed my work with one footstep. I just saw your coming and warned you in time. You have destroyed some of it already."

"Why do you do all this?" Aisha asked him.

"I have to hurry up, because when low tide comes I would certainly die. So I dig myself deep into the sand to protect myself from drying out. When high tide comes back, I can crawl out of my hole again."

Aisha tried her best to help repair what she destroyed; but as much as she tried hard, she was not successful. "Don't worry, I can do it all by myself", he said. But please look out where you walk next time!"
And he disappeared into his hole quickly and continued his work.

Quickly Aisha hurried back home as fast as her feet could carry her and told her mother what happened. "Well", said mother, "we human beings will never be able to do that what nature creates. This is why we must respect nature because we learn from her and without her we will never be able to live".

Aisha had her breakfast, Nasi Goreng (a malay rice dish)

"Time for school!" mother said and they left in a hurry.

At school Aisha told all her classmates and also to her teacher excitingly what she had experienced.

The iguana family

Aisha was playing with her girlfriends close to the jungle. She was busy splashing water on her friends. There was a beautiful waterfall (air terjun) nearby and the warm temperature invited playing in the water. The sun was already very high, school was over and the children were allowed to play outside after having finished their lunch which consisted of an egg (telur) and green beans (kacang hijau).

In the afternoon there was no school, because they had to help their parents. Then they started to play the telephone game.

They sat down in the warm sand. One of them started to tell a story and the next continued this story. After that the next child added more to that story and so on, until it was finished. So 5 children created some ideas out of the blue and ended up with a very nice and funny story.

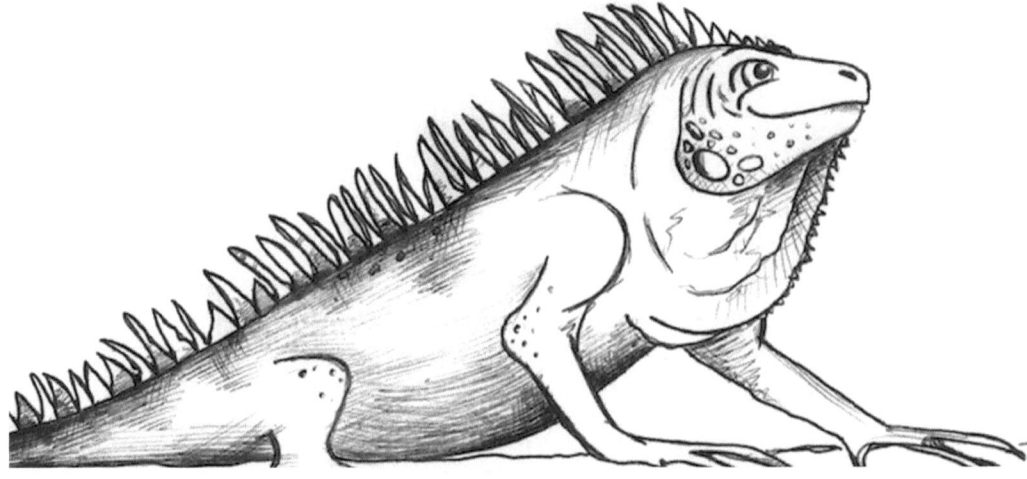

This is the story, which they made up:
Once upon a time there was an iguana which lived in the nearby jungle with his family. One day Saya Baruk, the father, found out that there was not enough food to feed his little family. Mother Mary also worked hard for food, collecting berries and little lizards and chewed them for her children in her mouth before feeding.

One day father met a little monkey which was swinging happily from branch to branch singing a nice song. He asked Tamtam, the monkey for help: "please, can you help us, my family is hungry and we cannot find enough food anymore. The people here cut all the trees and burn down the forest so that there is nothing to find anymore. Can you help us collect some fruit from the trees? I am too heavy and cannot climb up there myself".

Tamtam promised to help and called all of his friends. They carried Saya Buruk into the trees. From there the father was able to help himself and collect lots of small animals and fruit for his family. Then Tamtam and his friends brought him back down to the ground. Saya Buruk thought his experience was very tiring and difficult and did not want to ask the monkeys for anymore help.

Suddenly father iguana remembered that there was a village with people nearby. So he hurried to find them. It was a long way and he became very hungry. Arriving there, the people were frightened and ran away. But Sara Buruk did not want anything else but to beg for food. He did not want to frighten the people or to hurt them.

He entered the closest kitchen, helped himself and ate the most delicious food that was on the table. This kitchen belonged to the family of Aisha. There was really a lot of food, like Ayam (chicken), ikan biarawan (monkey fish), rumpai laut (sea weed) and cubis (cabbage). He enjoyed eating everything, it was so good! Mmmm! He was full than ever before in his life.

Then he looked for a bed to rest his tired body, dragging himself onto it, he covered himself with a blanket and fell asleep...

When Aisha came back, she found Saya Buruk sleeping in her bed! What a shock! She screamed loud for help...
Aisha had fallen asleep and had dreamt this ending. When she screamed aloud, her mother came running and took her into her arms and asked:
"What happened, my dear child?"

Aisha woke up and for a moment did not know where she was and whether she was asleep.

Mother smiled at her and told her, that it was just a dream. But for a long time her little heart kept beating very fast ...

Lissi

After having finished her homework Aisha layed down on the warm sand in front of her hut. She wanted to watch the clouds which slowly passed by in the sky.

She was trying to play the game "cloud theatre" seeing what figures they would make. She watched one cloud at a time until she was able to recognize different shapes. Then she made up a story using the shapes of those clouds.

One of the clouds looked like a little lamb, another like a bad fox, and another like a fairy. And so she invented a story: the bad wolf wanted to eat the little lamb, but the fairy used her magic on them and changed the bad wolf into a shepherd. So the lamb was safe, crawled out of its hiding place and the shepherd took care of the lovely fragile lamb.... So Aisha changed a bad story quickly into a good story and was happy about her success.

Suddenly something moved underneath her hand: oh my goodness, what was that? Quickly she withdrew her hand and looked what was there?

At first she thought it was a snake, but it was only a little lizard! She took a deep breath and was relieved. The lizard introduced herself: "I am Lissi, and you?" Aisha, still in shock told the lizard her name, as well. "I suggest, we play a little", said Lissi, I am so bored!" "Yes", answered Aisha, „come and play with me"!

Now Aisha had to explain her cloud game to Lissi and finally the new playmate understood. They were about to start.

Aisha and Lissi made up many funny stories. Lissi said. "I see a big fly"! And she tried to catch the fly jumping into the air. Ouch! She landed on her tummy and groamed and was disappointed that she was not able to catch the fly. The fly was not real, it existed only in her imagination." I do not want to continue this game," she said and licked her hearting tummy.

What a surprise! A fat fly sat directly on a rock in front of her. Quietly she approached the rock and snapped the fly, which was caught, in her mouth and Lissi enjoyed eating it.
Happy with her hurting tummy filled with a good meal the lizard lied down on the hot sand and enjoyed her meal.

Aisha watched her new friend's breathing for a while and touched her carefully. She found out that Lissi had a cold body. Well lizards are cold blooded, that is what she had learnt.

Aisha continued playing her favorite game watching clouds until mother called for lunch. The lizard, however, slept on and continued her fly meal.

Kingfisher Utam

Winter has come.

Winter in Malaysia means the rainy season. There is a dry season and a rainy season. During the rainy season father does not dare go fishing. The sea is too dangerous and the waves are very rough. So sometimes the family has to wait for a long time to get some fish. The only advantage in the rainy seasons is because it is not too hot and vegetables and fruit can grow properly in the fields. It can be very hot during the dry season, which is mainly between April and October. The children have many months of free time and Aisha looks forward to join her father when he goes fishing in the sea.
One day father went fishing in spite of the rough waves in order to catch fish for his family. There was not enough food at home.

He was just about throwing out his fishing line when a huge fish came out of the water and turned the boat upside down. Father and fishing line fell into the rough sea. Father was able to hold tight onto the boat´s edge but he did not know how to get back to shore. He was desperate and cried for help. But nobody could hear him the waves were too loud.

A kingfisher bird watched this whole episode and flew out to the hut of the family. He screamed so excitingly until he drew the family´s attention to himself. Of course Aisha was able to understand him. She knew the bird´s language; birds were her best friends! She quickly translated to her mother what the kingfisher had seen and had been trying to tell the family.

Finally mother believed the bird and noticed the turned-over boat far in the ocean and a man who is clinging tightly to its edge. She was scared to death because she recognized her husband and called the neighbors. She asked for help to get her husband out of the ocean, otherwise he would drown. Huge waves banged against the boat and threatened the grip of the man. Another big wave came and the man disappeared. He sank and sank, until a dolphin swam towards him. The man almost couldn't breathe anymore. With his last bit of strength he held onto the dolphin and together they reached the surface.

He looked into the eyes of the animal and cried: never ever in his life had he felt such love! And suddenly he was aware of his near death experience. Without the help of this dolphin he would have lost his life!

In the meantime his neighbors jumped into their boats in order to reach the drowning man. But even they had difficulties fighting against the high and dangerous waves, which banged ruthlessly against their boats.

Finally they came close to the man´s boat. The man´s face had already started turning blue and he was unable to speak because of all the water in his mouth and lungs. He did not want to let go of the dolphin because this wonderful creature had saved his life!

The helpful neighbors pulled him out of the water and exhausted he sank into the boat. He turned his head around to see the dolphin one more time. The dolphin jumped out of the water with joy once more and then disappeared...

With a huge effort the neighbors reached the shore with the rescued man just in time before another gigantic wave came.

Mother cried out for joy and thanked Aisha who had understood the words of Utam. She took her shivering husband into her arms and cried thankfully.
So this kingfisher Utam and a dolphin saved a human being!

Kingfishers wear a very beautiful color in their feathers and have a very long beak, which they use to catch fish. In spite of their beauty they scream loudly. But, as we have seen in this story, this loud cry was useful to warn the people.

Dolphins are so gentle and full of love. When you touch them you can feel a very warm experience. These animals love unconditionally and deserve the right of being respected!

Sea eagle Timor

And suddenly the sea eagle spread his wings and flew up into the air quickly as if he was in a hurry to leave the earth.

Yes, of course, he was in a hurry, very much in a hurry. His home, his tree was in danger because big waves turned up from the sea. Up above the top of the tree he had his nest: his 3 children were just about to hatch! He had to do something about it very quickly.

It was monsoon season and the rain didn't stop. It had been raining for weeks and the soil could not absorb the water. The earth is grateful for every drop of water, but these huge amounts of rain were too much. Therefore, the water started to rise and flooded the fields. Many people around the village Kuantan were in danger, the hut of Aisha's family as well.

„Help", called out Aisha´s little brother, „we are drowning!" and both of the other two brothers, Mohamed and Ibrahim were screaming as well.

Again and again big waves came nearer to the little house and water was pushing through the closed doors and windows. Mother panicked, but father remained calm.

Father watched Timor, the sea eagle, how lifted his wings and disappeared. Only he and Aisha knew what that meant. Aisha carefully watched the signs of the birds, as she learnt it from her father.

Both brothers carried big bags of sand and blocked up doors and windows. Many sand bags were already around the house and the family was able to rest for a while.

Very quietly father watched Timor and how he was circling around in the sky and was flying far over the ocean. His eyes followed Timor and he started to pray. He prayed for help. Aisha did the same. Both were very quiet and prayed. In their hearts there was hope for miracles. They strongly believed in miracles and knew that help was nearby.

Timor came back and with him a swarm of swallows. They flew in formation and directly towards the little house of Aisha´s parents. Aisha´s face was full of joy when she saw the birds coming. The birds then turned and flew into the next big wave of water. Some of them never came back.... Aisha knew what that meant and started to cry. The swallows had sacrificed their lives for the miracle.

The ocean was satisfied and a miracle happened: the waves became smaller and smaller. The ocean stopped sending its life-threatening waves to the shore. The sea had calmed down.

They were safe!!

Aisha and her family thanked the sea eagle and the numerous swallows, which were still alive and offered them food. Out of gratitude, Aisha`s father braced up the big tree on which the nest of the baby eagles was, so that the water was not able to uproot the tree. So the sea eagle was able to bring up his little family until they were able to spread their wings and fly.

Father, mother and children cried happily and fell into each other arms, very exhausted but relieved.

After some time the little birds flew off into the sky. Each Sunday they returned to the family, circled around the house and peeped gratefully down to them. Aisha and her father understood their language.

The talking trees

Once upon a time.. Aisha was born.

The parents and three brothers were happy about the arrival of the little girl! Their joy was so great that they invited all relatives and friends to celebrate this event.

Everyone came, even the hens, dogs and cats. Mother gave them what she could and was very generous even though she was so poor.

They were just happy!

Aisha smiled very early even though she was still small. Being in her buggy she was pushed outside under a banana tree by her mother for her nap. She looked at the tree and fell asleep.

She dreamt. She dreamt the banana tree would speak to her. No, she did not dream this at all the tree really spoke to her!

„Aisha, my sweet little one", the tree said, "come and fall asleep under my branches. I will sing for you".

And the tree murmured small melodies very quietly and Aisha fell asleep happily.

When she woke up she saw the smiling face of her mother and did not know whether it was mother who hummed all the time or whether it was the tree. She was too little to understand.

Mother took her out of her buggy, kissed her and gave her something to drink. Aisha was smiling all the time. It was as if she was dreaming. She turned her little head towards the tree, back to her mother, back to the tree. She did not remember anymore which it was.

Later, when she started to talk she asked her mother whether a tree is able to speak. But her mother only smiled and kept quiet. Mother did not want to answer many questions because she wanted Aisha to have her own experiences.

Now, when Aisha became 7 years old, she was sure that trees could speak.

Many times she strolls around the jungle, very quietly, and listened to the words of the trees. Some had a very deep voice, some of them a very high voice. Some grumbles and some hummed. When she came back from her adventurous tours she told her banana tree

under which she had been so many times being small.
Her banana tree had now become a big tree.

She hugged him – because he remained her favorite
tree, after all.

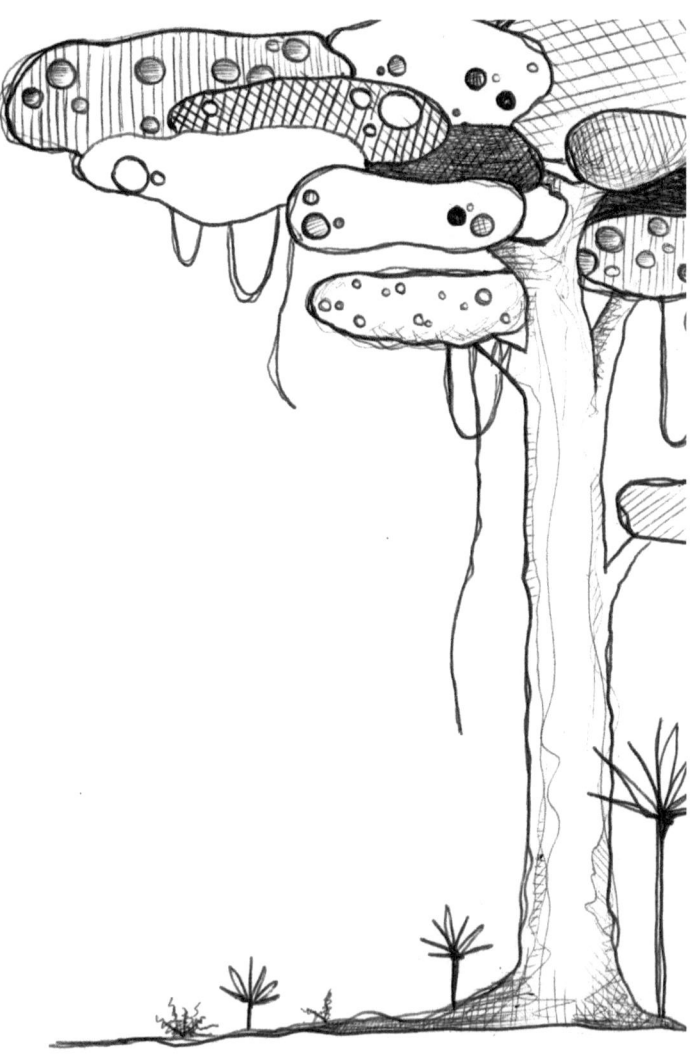

Grandmother

The muezzin is the singer in the minaret, which is a tower of a mosque, and he had just finished praying aloud to the world around him. The day had started even though it was still dark out. It takes just a few minutes for dawn to vanish and the city lights to be turned off.

The birds begin to sing. The beautiful blue kingfisher birds scream aloud "selamat bagi" which means "hello", the sea eagles circle above the ocean and get ready for the day.
Aisha was preparing for school, the brothers had already left the house already, mother was beginning to clean away after breakfast dishes and father had also left for work.

Suddenly two horses seemed to appear at the horizon: they grew larger as they came closer.

Aisha was frightened at first. When they got closer, Aisha recognized one of the riders: it was her grandmother, and she looked so young!

But – that's impossible, Aisha thought, my grandmother passed away many years ago!

She died during a thunderstorm. It happened when she was in the garden, a flash of lightening hit the nearby tree under which grandmother was resting and she died. Grandmother was then still very young and Aisha was only a year old. Everything happened so fast.

Now this is what people told her.
But what really happened, nobody was able to say. Grandmother was suddenly gone, disappeared from the earth. No one ever saw her again.
That happened many years ago.

And now – what is this? Is this really grandmother?? Sitting on a horse with a companion beside her?

Aisha! What is happening in your head?
She called out aloud: „grandma, is that you?"

The woman, whom she thought was grandmother, smiled and got off the horse. She hugged Aisha warmly and sat down in the sand and started to tell her what had happened and why she was here.

She said that long time ago a flash of lightening came down from heaven and carried her up into the sky. After a long journey they came into a different country. The houses were made of cotton. Beds made of whipped cream, everywhere there were trees and flowers that looked gold.

The people there had wings and look very kind. She decided to stay in this country because she liked it there very much. After some time, however, she started to feel homesick and wished to visit her family again. This wish was now fulfilled. They gave her two horses and a companion. Of course the horses had wings so that they could fly down from heaven.

Grandmother told this to Aisha with a smile in her face so that Aisha had tears in her eyes as she hugged her. She loved her grandmother very much and had missed her for such a long time.

They were sitting there for a long time as they hugged each other.

When Aisha opened her eyes again she was surprised being held by her mother and not by her grandmother! What had happened?

She told her mother what she had experienced; but mother smiled: „Aisha, my love, your grandmother was certainly with you. I am sure she missed you. You see how lovely it is when you believe in miracles!

Come on, get ready for school. "
With a big sigh Aisha understood that she had been dreaming all the time because she missed her grandmother so very much and her dream had become true.
When she looked around, both riders had disappeared as if they had never existed.

But the strong feeling, when her grandmother held her, she never forgot.
And sometimes she would sit by the sea where it all had happened, closed her eyes and dreamt of her beloved grandmother again.

Where do the pigs come from??

Night has begun. The sun has set and the first lights of the town were about to be turned on. Aisha helped her mother to clean up the kitchen because the family was finished dinner. They had had a delicious mee (rice dish) with lots of vegetables. Fresh pineapple from the garden was their dessert.

Mother washed the dishes and Aisha dried them, which was what little girls usually do. The three boys helped father to repair the path to the house because large flooding destroyed it a couple of weeks ago and almost the house went with it. It took a long time until everything was put into order again.

From the corner of his eye Mohamed suddenly saw a shadow: he looked carefully: 5 pigs walked by. The big one first followed by 4 little ones. Quietly grunting they passed by and tried to disappear. Father lifted up his gun and aimed at the big one.

It was a mother pig looking for food for her little ones. She suddenly spoke and asked the father not to shoot. She had been on her way for such a long time and had become very hungry. "If you shoot me, my kids must die of hunger. They are too young to find their own food!" And as she spoke the little ones ran away each one into a different direction.

Frightened the father dropped his gun. He did not expect that pigs were able to talk! He looked at the mother pig without moving. He would have had the chance to shoot her, but he was still too shocked and could not pick up his gun again.

Mother pig said: "you should not hunt us. We are fat pigs which is not good for you people to eat. Why don't you grow vegetables, fruit and grain instead? Eating us is not healthy for you because it will make you ill. You will regret it very soon.

„We can help by digging holes" she continued and called her kids back.

„Look, when you keep us as pets we can help digging holes and you can plant trees into those holes. We can work together with you."

Father did not mind accepting that offer and put his gun back into the house.

He built a fence and the animals were allowed to stay with the family. When their help was needed they helped digging. He was convinced that he made the right decision.

In the meantime the sun had set and a wonderful sunset colored the sky, bats began to fly around, the birds stopped singing and the cicadas went to sleep.
How peaceful can it be when people and animals live peacefully and respect each other!

Since that day father has never ever killed an animal and his health has gotten better from day to day, because he eats better.

The adventures of Ayer Ketam

"Well, that would be too easy", Ayer Ketam said to himself, "if someone would dig in my hole trying to pull me out"!

He tried to hide back in his hole and grinned foolishly from ear to ear. Again a crab catcher was standing in front of his hole and let a stick down into the hole and tried to catch him.

The local people catch crabs by putting a long stick into a crab hole and wait for the crab to hold on to it. When they feel the crab has taken hold of the stick they very slowly pull out the stick. If they pull out the stick too fast, they lose him.

It was Mohamed, the big brother of Aisha who was putting the stick into the hole. Mohamed murmured something strange to himself, but Ayer Ketam heard him. He called up to him: "let me live! You will still be hungry when you eat me, because there is not much to my body. You might even break a tooth by trying to eat me!"

"I promise to bring you to a wonderful place where you will find the most delicious fruit which you may have and bring to your family. But you must let me live!"

Mohamed was shocked, because he never heard a crab speaking before! He listened carefully and so the crab repeated his words. Very clearly he now understood that the voice came out of the hole where the crab was.

Still confused about the voice he called down into the hole: „Alright, I promise not to kill you. But you must also keep your promise". So he let the stick down into the hole, the crab held tight to it and Mohamed pulled him out.

Now they looked into each other´s eyes. Ayer Ketam was not sure whether this man would keep his promise and had chills running up and down his back. Mohamed hesitated for a moment and was not sure whether he should kill the crab or not. But since he belonged to Aisha´s family he was used to being honest and so he let the crab go. The crab then ran as fast as he could and Mohamed followed him.

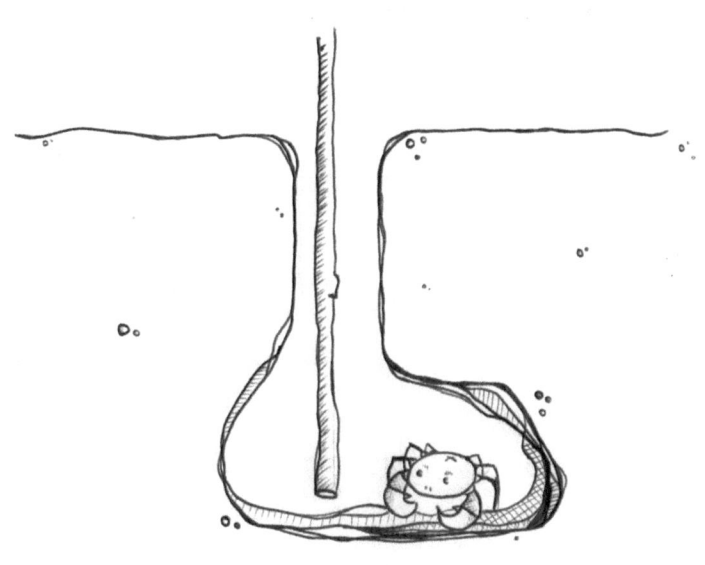

After half an hour of running– the sun had risen into the sky and Mohamed was sweating – they arrived: What did his eyes see?

In front of him there was a garden, it was a heavenly garden. There were dozens of fruit trees with ripe fruits. The ground was covered with pineapples and green vegetables. He never saw such a beautiful garden! In the middle of the garden stood a girl with golden hair, smiling to him and said: "You see, I will give you all these things in my garden because you did not kill the crab", and she reached out to him, took him around so that he could help himself.

Very happily he returned home with his arms full of delicious fruits and vegetables.

Aisha came to meet him and he couldn't wait to tell what he had experienced.

He never saw Ayer Ketam ever again – did the crab really talk to him? Well, obviously he did.... Otherwise, where did all the fruits and vegetables come from that he brought home on his arms picked from the most beautiful garden he had ever seen in his life?

The swallows

Once again dark and black clouds appeared in the sky! It is still the rainy season and "the tail of the rain is again moving before he starts to withdraw" – the end of the season is coming soon.

Swallows fly in circles.

Aisha watched them from her window and finally she goes outside to watch them better. Suddenly there is restlessness amongst them. They are communicating with each other:

"Let`s fly away quickly, a heavy rain will start soon!" and they try to reach the shoreline. They need to use their wings because there are no air currents anymore. They look almost like bats; Aisha has to look carefully in order to see the difference.

Rain suddenly starts very heavily.

And suddenly a very small swallow has turned around, his little wings give out and he is seen no more. Maybe his little wings were wet or he had no flight experience? Aisha has tears in her eyes as she looks out for the bird in the ocean. She finds it no more....

Now the little swallow has found its peace in the deep ocean. Aisha cries. She cries even more when she saw that two bigger swallows flew in circles over the spot where the little one had disappeared. The big swallows cried out loud, but in vain.

So nature has taken its course.

All other swallows fled in time and were safe.
After some time the heavy rain stopped, only a few drops fell down from the sky and the birds started to sing again. Maybe their songs were meant to announce the end of the rain? Or is the singing a mourning for the little swallow? We do not know.

Sadly the little swallow died because it had too much courage to fly far out over the ocean. Maybe he was too curious and adventurous. Maye he just enjoyed to fly and forgot about the rainstorm.

We only know that swallows announce the coming of a rain when they fly very low. When they fly high, the weather if fine.

And Aisha dried her tears...

The disguise

Aisha was asleep in her bed. All around her, it was quiet.

Suddenly a heavy rainfall woke her up. The ocean had been calmed down and tide was at its highest. Rain fell endlessly. The noise was so loud that it was impossible for Aisha to fall asleep again.

She felt itchy. Had she forgotten to properly put the mosquito net around her bed? It had to be attached tightly under the mattress so that the mosquitos could not find her. In fact she had spread the net only loosely around her bed this time. So it was her fault. She had lit a mosquito coil (repellent), but it did not work well enough. She asked herself, why had God created such insects; what good do they do. They only bother us. They land on our skin and animal as well. They hold tightly as they sting us and their poison flows into our bodies as they suck out blood. That does not seem to be a very good idea!

Aisha got up and sipped some water from her glass. Then she sat down onto a chair and listened to the falling rain. She hoped that all animals had found a protected place so that they were dry from the rain. Her eyes were closing because she was so sleepy and half asleep she heard the mosquitos buzzing. Suddenly the buzzing changed into voices. These dark creatures turned into little stars. Those stars multiplied and flew to the hungry animals

The heavy rain changed into a light drizzle and gave all animals to drink.
Aisha woke up suddenly because she almost fell off the chair and the water glass in her hand had tipped over on her legs.

She jumped up and went to bed again and was very happy about her dream: the changing of the rain into drinking water for the animals and the mosquitos changing into food for them.
At least the mosquitos had fulfilled a good purpose for the world.

The surprise

Night had fallen.

The little monkeys were swinging swiftly on the trees, a swallow hurried home, the cicadas stopped humming and the bats had begun their night flight. The ocean was quiet and it was dark now.

Aisha kissed her mom and dad good night and disappeared into her room to set her school bag ready for the next day.

She quickly undressed and slipped into her nightgown, washed her face and brushed her teeth. She was looking forward to go to bed since she had had a hard day. Coming back from school she had to help her parents work in the fields all that afternoon. People were expecting rain quite soon and the seed that was planted in the soil would soon open and growing into grain.

She jumped into her cozy bed, said her prayer and closed her eyes.

Suddenly she heard some noise in her room!
It was near her school bag and she could hear it rustling! She listened. There was that noise again! Maybe it was a gecko. She waited a little while and did not dare to switch on the light. Again there was rustling this time from a different corner. What could that be? Now it sounded that someone was eating noisily and Aisha's heart started to beat very fast. She could not guess what this noise was all about. She decided to wait a little longer. Surely it was not a burglar, because mom and dad were still up and the house was full of light. But what in the world was that noise in her room??

The tension was too much and she switched on her flashlight very quietly under the blanket. She then turned the flashlight quickly towards the direction where the noise had came from. Oh, a hedgehog was making that noise! He was so frightened when Aisha looked at him with big eyes that his food almost fell out of his mouth.

„I am sorry, Aisha", the hedgehog said. "I was so hungry and took your sandwich out of your school bag."
What? This creature was talking to Aisha and thought this was very natural that a hedgehog could speak.
„But who are you really?"

„Of course", Aisha said, „you entered my room, opened my school bag, took out my school sandwich and started to eat"!
„But who are you really"?

After all what Aisha has already experienced she was already used to the fact that an animal could speak and that miracles can happen.

„O, I suppose you would like to hear that I am a prince in disguise or something like that, eh?"
The hedgehog answered. „But I am sorry to say that I am a very simple hedgehog and that I was hungry!"

„And how were you able to open my school bag, take out my sandwich and start eating as we do?" Aisha asked him.

„Because… because…. Because…" answered the hedgehog.

Suddenly her younger brother Zainiffa appeared behind her desk and grinned from ear to ear.

„You silly one, why did you frighten me!" Aisha screamed at him, „don't you have something better to do than to play games with me?"

Zainiffa laughed and was very happy that he had been able to fool his sister. He had caused those noises, he had opened the school bag and he had changed his voice. And he quickly ran out of the room.
Now the hedgehog looked at Aisha for a very long time and said: „I suppose you are really not sure that it was me that was talking to you, or not??
Who do you think was talking to Aisha: the brother or the hedgehog?

Thanks to all the people who helped publishing this book, especially

Beate Melzer
Raymond Eiber
Jan Anderson
Emely Weipert
Narina Eiber
And all the others who supported this book.
Thank you!

FSC
www.fsc.org

MIX

Papier aus ver-
antwortungsvollen
Quellen
Paper from
responsible sources

FSC® C105338